Mrs Whitlam

Mrs Whitlam

BRUCE PASCOE

This is a Magabala Book

LEADING PUBLISHER OF ABORIGINAL AND
TORRES STRAIT ISLANDER STORYTELLERS.

CHANGING THE WORLD, ONE STORY AT A TIME.

First published 2016, reprinted 2017 x2, 2019
Revised 2019, reprinted 2021, 2023
Magabala Books Aboriginal Corporation, Broome, Western Australia
Website: www.magabala.com Email: sales@magabala.com

Magabala Books receives financial assistance from the Commonwealth Government through the Australia Council, its arts advisory body. The State of Western Australia has made an investment in this project through the Department of Local Government, Sport and Cultural Industries. Magabala Books would like to acknowledge the support of the Shire of Broome, Western Australia.

Magabala Books is Australia's only independent Aboriginal and Torres Strait Islander publishing house. Magabala Books acknowledges the Traditional Owners of the Country on which we live and work. We recognise the unbroken connection to traditional lands, waters and cultures. Through what we publish, we honour all our Elders, peoples and stories, past, present and future.

Original internal design Tracey Gibbs
This edition cover & design Jo Hunt

Printed and bound by Griffin Press, South Australia

9781925936346 (paperback)

A catalogue record for this book is available from the National Library of Australia

♥

For Marnie,
Mrs Whitlam (the horse and the woman),
Gillian Mears, Rachel Womanbird and Quinn

One

'What's your name?'

'Marnie.'

The woman looked from the girl to her hands holding the teacup.

'Marnie,' she paused. 'They say you can ride.'

'Yeah — a bit.'

'Mr Marriner says you ride very well but you don't have a horse.'

I shrugged my shoulders. Of course I didn't have a horse.

'Would you be able to look after a horse, Marnie? Feed it? Groom it? Keep it shod?' I shrugged again.

'Where would you keep a horse?'

'Mr Marriner said I could keep it with his — if I ever got one.' I knew what Mrs Arnold was getting at but it was taking a while. Even so I was trying not to hope too much.

'I have a horse here which I need taken good care of. She's been … well looked after and ridden every day.' Mrs Arnold stopped and looked down at her hands which were twisting the teacup, grinding it softly on the saucer.

'She's a good horse, Marnie. She needs to be well looked after … loved. She's used to being loved.'

Well we all need that.

'Her name is Mrs Margaret Whitlam. You might think it's a silly name but she is a beautiful horse — big and bold. Nothing scares her, she'll jump anything for you.'

You. You … I hoped.

'You can have Mrs Whitlam. The saddle, bridle, halter, blankets, rugs, combs.' Mrs Arnold thought for a moment. 'Helmet, boots, jodhpurs. The lot. Have you somewhere to keep these things?'

Uh-oh, I thought, she's seen our house, maybe even heard about my family.

'Mr Marriner said if I got a horse I could keep all the gear in his tack room.'

'Yes, he's a nice man. I asked him about you.' Mrs Arnold went back to twisting the cup. She stayed silent for a while. The grating of cup against saucer was getting on my nerves.

'My daughter is dead, you know.'

Of course I knew, she went to the same school as me.

'I can't have the horse here or the gear. I can't … '

She stopped twisting the cup as if realising for the first time what she'd been doing.

'So, Marnie, I'd be very grateful if you could take the horse away today. I can't help you. I hope you understand. I don't want to see the horse again. Please don't ride her past here. I couldn't bear to see her. My daughter loved Maggie so much.'

I nodded, hoping Mrs Arnold would see that I understood and not start bawling.

Two

She was right. Everything was there. Mrs Whitlam was mouthing my fist with big, soft, bristly lips. I looked at the gear hanging from the pegs in the stable. The boots were the cutest things I had ever seen. And that riding hat — dark blue velvet. It made my stomach wriggle to think of feeling that in my hands. I felt like a thief. But Mrs Arnold had asked me and in the end I could see she was *begging* me to take the horse and all the things — to get them out of her sight.

I took the halter off a peg and Mrs Whitlam's big eyes followed me. She looked me straight in the eye as I drew the halter over her ears and clipped the lead rope to the ring. She threw her head up and showed me the whites of her eyes.

'Look, Mrs Whitlam, Mrs Arnold said I've got to look after you. Vicki's gone. You know that. So you're coming with me. No use hanging around here with no one coming out of the house to even say hello.'

The horse looked down at me. When I held the bridle under her chin, she accepted the bit like an angel. She even stood patiently as I saddled her up and tightened her girth. I stuffed as much tack as I could in my backpack and tied the rest of the gear to the two rings at the back of the saddle.

My stomach gave a surge as I imagined tying a saddlebag to those rings and riding along the river to swim her. And having a barbecue afterwards. I couldn't believe it. It was a dream. An incredible dream with me, Marnie Clark, on a horse — and the whole world to ride it in.

I could compete in the show, take Maggie to pony club … I could … I shook my head. Get the horse over to Mr Marriner and then start to dream. I could keep working at the chemist to pay for the hard feed and the vet and … *ugh, come on, get on with it*. Take the horse out of Mrs Arnold's sight. Poor thing, she was going mad. Ever since her daughter was killed in that car crash.

I pressed my face into Mrs Whitlam's neck, tears rolled down my cheeks. I was hoping they were for Vicki but really, I knew most of them were for me.

I decided to walk her over to her new home. I held the reins loosely and Maggie followed along but tossed her head every now and then with her eyes rolling, trying to glance back at the paddock.

'Come on, old Maggie, you'll like it over at Bimbi Park. We'll look after you real good. You know Mr Marriner is the best horseman around here. He'll help me take care of you.'

I looked down at the huge, hairy feet of the horse. Everyone knew Maggie had Clydesdale in her. Even when Vicki had ridden her, some of the girls had laughed at Maggie's big feet and huge bum.

'It doesn't matter Maggie. Everyone knows that you're the fastest horse in the sand — even faster than Flicker, Sarah Valentino's racehorse.' Flicker. I scoffed at the name but then thought of Mrs Whitlam.

I kicked at the stones as we walked along, the horse's breath puffing warmly on my hair. Every now and then I could feel her soft rubbery lips and whiskers just touch my ear. The horse was doing it deliberately. I'm here, Marnie, don't forget me.

She needed to be loved, this great heavy-footed horse. And I could love her. I could love this horse, Maggie, and defy anyone to laugh. I'd fight them rather than let them laugh at *my* horse … even her name. I'd love to call her Cloud or Windrush or Willow or Riverstone, anything but Mrs Whitlam. I knew my mother would have something to say about that. *You're thinking of yourself. What about the horse? She thinks she* is *Mrs Whitlam. Change her name and how's the poor thing going to feel?*

So Mrs Margaret Whitlam it would have to be. Maggie. I'd just call her Maggie and maybe people would forget the Mrs Whitlam bit. I knew what Mum would say about that too. *You should be proud to have a horse named after that lady — she was a wonderful woman, her old man wasn't a bad bloke either, even if he was Prime Minister. Did a bit for black people too. More than most of them!*

Mum talked like that a fair bit. She left school at twelve but she was smart. She knew everything that was going on. If you got up in the middle of the night you'd find her reading the newspaper. She read every word: car accidents, deaths, famous divorces, unlikely marriages, discoveries of half alligator-half humans in the North American Everglades, political and world news. The only thing she wouldn't read was the business page. *What's the good of reading about money when you got none? Like talkin' about pancakes when the kitchen cupboards got nothin' but dead cockroaches and starving mice.* She talked like that, my mum.

And now Marnie Clark of Curdie Vale had a horse. The horse was a Clydesdale and had a strange name but she was mine and what's more she was quite prepared to allow me to love her, to let me press my face into the hard muscles of her neck and feel the warmth of her chestnut hair.

Yep, the horse that used to belong to a dead girl. I had never really known Vicki. We went to the same school and lived in the same district but Vicki was older. She mixed with the pony club kids and the families with flash cars and holiday houses. But now I had a horse too and if Mr Marriner had room in his float I'd be able to ride at the Warrnambool Show. Who cares if the judges laughed when they saw a Clydesdale jumping fences!

I remembered seeing a show on TV, where a Clydesdale galloped beside a river and leapt over a log. This was how I imagined Mrs … er, Maggie, would look with Marnie Clark on her back riding up to get the blue ribbon. And I'd hang the ribbon in my bedroom and if any of my brothers touched it, I'd open our birdcage and let their canaries go. My brothers loved their canaries. What did they call them? The golden birds of song. They got that off my father. He had plenty of time to think up stuff like that. He was still looking for work and was always dreaming of winning the lottery or whatever else he dreamed about.

Three

'Hey Clarky, what you doin' with that carthorse? Goin' out to plough the paddock are ya?'

I should have been watching where I was going instead of daydreaming. Should have seen those boys coming from a kilometre away.

And Stevenson was with them. He always made a comment about the colour of my skin or my family. Stinky Stevenson he was called, ever since he filled his pants in primary school. My brothers reminded him of it every time I told them he'd been teasing me.

'Hey, Stinky, how heavy are ya jocks brah?' they'd call out to him in front of his mates.

Maggie flinched as the first stone skidded underneath her. The next one hit her on the flank and she threw her head back.

'Carthorse, carthorse,' Stinky yelled as he picked up another big stone.

Maggie was still hauling herself back and her eyes were looking wild. She might break free, run back to Vicki's house and then Mrs Arnold might scream and say stuff like I couldn't look after her. She might take Maggie off me and give her to someone else — someone who already *had* a horse.

I hardly had time to think what to do before I found myself doing it. I grabbed hold of Maggie's mane, put my foot in the stirrup, and hoisted myself up onto her back. I kept the reins short and gave Maggie a little rap with my heels. One hand on the reins and the other knotted in the mane, I charged her back through the boys who, seeing the great beast bearing down on them, leapt the church hedge.

I trotted away smugly but not before I heard Stinky yell out, 'Carthorse, carthorse, dark horse, darky's horse.'

I turned Maggie around again and rode back to the boys who, stupidly, thought it was safe to come back on the footpath.

This time Maggie was in stride and understood the game. She arched her regal neck and made sure her feet came down on the road like clattering claps of thunder. It wasn't the clip-clop, clip-clop, like the nice horses in storybooks. It was the club-clap club-clap clubbidy-clappity club-clap like the mighty warrior horse she was. It must have sounded like the detonations of bombs and the boys took off like scared rabbits.

I brought my face down to rest on Maggie's neck as I walked her along the creek behind the footy oval. She was warm as toast and had that wonderful horsey smell that you woke up in the middle of the night thinking about. What a horse!

I thought of Mrs Arnold who had lost her daughter and of Vicki, who had lost everything including this mighty horse. I began to cry. What could I ever do to honour Vicki's memory and how could I thank Mrs Arnold?

My heart was beating as strongly as Maggie's. I was so lucky and so in love with this horse that already seemed to understand exactly what I wanted her to do.

Four

Mr Marriner had a riding school on the other side of the creek. I stopped under a big gum tree to look across at his farm and the paddock where he said I could keep a horse — if I ever got one. He'd painted all the sheds in the brown and gold of our local footy team.

The farm looked beautiful in the late afternoon sun, the white fences and the lush green grass of the creek flats. Luck, luck, I had it all. No one had any idea how good my life was at this moment.

I thought about getting off to walk Maggie through the creek, it was only centimetres deep, but on a day like this you ride your luck. I urged Maggie into the water and the big horse strode through it as proud as a queen.

'I saw those kids from the hill,' Mr Marriner called out as I rode into the yard. 'Saw you ride through them. They came past here like they were training for the hundred metre sprint. Mind you, Marnie, that wasn't a good idea, a horse you didn't know. She could have done anything, reared, shied, bolted. Don't let me see you doing that when you take kids out on a ride for me. There's rules you know. You've gotta behave yourself. I can't have people thinkin' this riding school's a race track!'

I turned Maggie toward the yards.

'Did you hear me? You'll have to make that horse love you. Getting her into a trot is one thing, getting her to respect you is another. And you'll have to work on it. I don't want no rogues here.'

I slipped down from the saddle. It was a bit like sliding off an elephant. I felt small again beside such a horse. My face just reached the muscle of her shoulder, which was glistening with sweat and flickering under the fine red hide as she relaxed. Gee, she was a beautiful animal.

Vicki's mum said Maggie wasn't scared of anything and neither was I. Well, I had been sometimes but with a horse like this it'd have to be something pretty awful to make me scared again.

I was pretty full of myself as I led Maggie into the yard. I squeezed between her and the fence post and felt the enormous power of her shoulder. She could crush you without knowing it. She'd have to remember that I was there or I'd get hurt. Maggie would have to be aware of everything I did and everywhere she put her feet. I'd have to teach her that. Mr Marriner didn't make idle threats, one hint of rogue behaviour and she'd be out the gate.

'Here,' Mr Marriner was at my shoulder. 'Here's some sugar cubes. Wait until she wanders away and then call her back. Give her the sugar and walk away, give her another one if she follows you. Do it every day for ten days and on day two give her sugar every third time she comes when you call. Right?'

Of course it was right. I knew the rules but I also knew that ten days of teaching my horse was never going to be a problem. I wanted her to love me, not just do what she was told. I wanted a mate.

Five

'She give you that horse, then?' my mother asked as she was making hamburgers on the stove. She called them rissoles but us kids said the only way to make them sound interesting was to call them hamburgers.

Dad was sitting at the table trying to fix another clock. For want of something to do he picked things up at the tip and repaired them. We all had bikes with mismatched wheels and pedals, footballs and basketballs with patched bladders, and my youngest brother Eric even wore a beanie and jumper from a rival football team.

'Well?' Mum asked. 'Did she give you that girl's horse?'

'Yes, she's over at Mr Marriner's. Helmet and clothes too. Good saddle and tack.'

'Is she quiet?' Mum asked, turning from the stove.

'She's beautiful, Mum. She does everything you say. She's not scared of anything.'

'You'll have to thank that lady.'

'She said she never wanted to see the horse again. She's real upset.'

'Wouldn't any mother be?' said Mum, turning the hamburgers as they sizzled in the pan. 'But we'll have to thank her somehow.'

'She could have one of my clocks,' Dad said, giving the one he was working on a cautious wind.

'Um … it's not that kind of house, Dad. Everything's new and it's all neat and tidy, like no one lives there.'

'Hmmm, well there's someone missing from that house. Make any place look empty I reckon,' Mum said softly.

'Anyway, she's beautiful. Mrs Whitlam her name is. Maggie for short.'

'Mrs Whitlam,' said Dad. 'Who'd give a horse a name like that?'

Mum brought a huge plate of hamburgers and toasted buns to the table. My brothers turned up and in the chaos of voices and scraping chairs, the hamburgers vanished.

'What about your poor old mother?' Mum sighed.

'Yes, you kids, what about your poor old mother?' Dad chuckled through a huge mouthful of bun.

'Anyway,' Mum said ignoring Dad and turning to me. 'If she's called Mrs Whitlam, then that's that. If the horse thinks that's her name then you can't go confusing the poor beast by calling her something else. She's had enough upsets for the time being.'

Spot on, just what I thought she'd say. Just then, the first of the clocks in the house began to strike the hour. This continued on for another ten minutes with all of Dad's second-hand clocks chiming in with their idea of the right time, although none of them ever agreed.

When all the clocks had had their say, Dad leaned forward. 'So, where ya gonna go first?'

'Down the river but I thought I might go down to pony club tomorrow afternoon. See how she goes around the course, see how she gets on with the other horses.'

'She would've known 'em horses from when the other girl was riding her,' Dad said in his most reasonable voice.

'Well I think it's a great idea,' Mum chipped in. 'You can get used to each other before going to the river.'

I had a mouthful of burger and suddenly it seemed like I'd bitten into the whole cow. I chewed it slowly. I said that about pony club without really thinking. I had just wanted to keep Mum and Dad talking about *my* horse. Once I said it, I knew I would have to go. Mum wouldn't let me ride to the river on my own.

Six

My hands shook as I put the bridle on Maggie after school. She rolled the bit in her mouth until it was comfortable and then nuzzled into my neck. This time when I swung the saddle over the saddle blanket, Maggie looked around to check that I knew what I was doing.

'Well you tell me if there's a special way,' I said to her, my face pressed into the barrel of her body, secretly breathing in her horsiness. 'I want you to be comfortable. We're going to pony club … where your mates are.'

Maggie puttered through her lips and shifted her feet as I cinched up the girth.

'I'll look after you, Maggie.' Really I was praying she would look after me.

We rode down the lane to the road. Mr Marriner looked up from the pump he was fixing in the paddock, and shielded his eyes from the glare of the sun. He waved to me and when I looked back he was still squinting into the sun, watching me.

Long before I got to the white rails of the pony club, I could hear the girls calling out to each other and laughing. I slowly turned into the gate. It felt like everyone went quiet and still. I didn't know whether they were admiring or laughing at me.

Indie Moorehouse walked her horse, Bandit, towards us. 'What are you doing?' she asked.

'I'm taking Maggie around the course. Mr Marriner said I could.'

'Mr Marriner, what would he know?' she replied.

There was nothing I could say. I was breathless with tension. I gave Maggie the softest heel and pulled the reins ever so slightly, even though my hands were shaking. Maggie turned away from Indie and Bandit and walked on. Regal was the word that would come to me later.

'And did Mr Marriner say you could ride Vicki's horse?' I heard Indie call out loudly enough for all the girls to hear.

'Maggie's mine now. Her mother gave her to me,' I managed to say, even though my throat was as tight as a cinch strap.

'And her clothes?'

I pretended not to hear and trotted away. All I wore that belonged to Vicki were her riding pants that I'd rolled up because they were too long.

Maggie began the course and wove stolidly through the tyre maze. She cleared the coloured poles like she was stepping over a crack in the footpath. It was a breeze. Coming through the water basin, her big feet sent up an embarrassing amount of water.

I turned and rode back towards the others. No one said a word. I looked over at the more friendly faces but even they were silent, cowed by the bossy presence of Indie Moorehouse.

I knew my voice was not reliable enough to speak so I rode on toward the gate but not before I overheard someone say, ' … Vicki's clothes … ' They were the kind of words that hung in the air. What I knew for sure was that I wasn't coming back.

Maggie's step was as sure and determined as my voice wasn't. Perhaps she had made up her mind she wasn't going back either.

Mr Marriner had finished working on the pump and as I rode up the lane, I wiped my cheeks with my sleeve to get rid of the tears I'd tried to squeeze away.

Maggie turned her head and nudged my foot. She could have been shooing a botfly but she was looking right at me. She truly was my horse.

I dragged the saddle off Maggie, having to stand on tiptoe to reach high enough, stored the tack on the hooks and scooped a tin of oats out of the bin. I was allowed seven scoops a week as part of my pay.

'How'd it go?' Mr Marriner asked, scaring the daylights out of me. He was leaning against the tack rail.

'Here,' he offered a glass. 'I opened a bottle of lemonade and can't finish it. Bit gassy for me.'

I took the glass gratefully. I would have had my face in Maggie's trough if it weren't for the precious lemonade.

'So, how'd it go?' Mr Marriner asked again.

I had to straighten myself and take another sip from the glass to be sure my voice wouldn't wobble.

'Good … yeah, good,' I managed.

'Greet ya with open arms did they?'

My chest heaved and I took another gulp of the drink. 'I, I … ' but I couldn't find anything to say that he'd believe, so I sat down with a plop on the boot rail with the wind knocked right out of me.

'Indie, was it?'

I nodded. So did he.

'I taught her how to ride, you know.'

I nodded again.

'I've watched her over the years, growing up. She always has to find a way of being the best. She's not a bad kid but not as far as her dad is concerned. You ever see her with him?'

I shook my head.

'Her dad is a businessman, he's on council, all that sort of thing. He always wanted a son you see and he didn't get one.'

Maggie came over and put her face through the fence, all whiskers and oat dust. She nudged me under the armpit, nearly knocking me off the rail.

'Know what that means, Marnie?' asked Mr Marriner. 'That means she's happy. Happy to have been out and about, happy to have someone to look after her, happy to have someone to love.' He tousled Maggie's shaggy mane and inspected it.

'Few bot eggs in here you'll have to get before you go home. No, you're a lucky girl Marnie, love all along the line. Not everyone has that.'

He poured more lemonade into my glass and looked across the paddocks.

'Do you remember Silver, Indie's horse before she got Bandit?'

I vaguely remembered another horse but Indie was older than me.

'Well, Indie was riding that little grey in the gymkhana. It was her and another girl from Simpson riding for the blue ribbon. Silver refused the last barrel rail. When Indie got to the yards, her father told her to get out of the saddle. He jumped on Silver's back and made that pony pay all the way to Camperdown. I saw them coming back, poor little Silver's eyes were like dinner plates, she had foam all along her withers. I stopped my ute and got out to have a chat but he went right past, turned around and called me a few swear words. Well, I think they were swear words, I hadn't heard half of them before.'

I drank the last of the lemonade and tried to keep my hat on as Maggie nibbled at the brim.

'I turned around and followed them back. He let Silver into the paddock and screamed at that poor pony. Indie just sobbed. Never seen a horse so broken. He was quivering from hock to heel.'

Mr Marriner went into the shed and brought back a comb. 'Here, get into that mane, it'll calm both of you down.'

I heard his footsteps crunch across the gravel and soon I could hear the broom at work behind the feed shed.

I ran the comb through Maggie's mane and discovered the bot eggs, which I should have noticed earlier when I put on her bridle. She turned her head and mouthed my wrist with her soft lips. I leant my face into her neck and made it all wet.

Seven

At dinner that night, in the quiet created by full mouths and the lull of chiming clocks, I daydreamed about Maggie and our first big ride on Saturday. I planned what I would wear, what food I'd take, what treats I'd bring for Maggie, what kids to invite and what tracks we'd follow from the river down to the sea. The ride to the coast would be a canter beneath the overhanging wattles and eucalypts of the riverbank. It would be the biggest adventure I had ever been on.

'So, how did pony club go?' Mum asked, shattering my dream.

'Not bad,' I responded slowly.

'Not what Mr Marriner said.'

'Did he ring you?' I asked, suddenly panicked that Mr Marriner was on my case.

'No, I rang him.'

'Why?'

'I'm your mother. I was a young girl in this town too you know. I know how it goes and I know what some of those girls can be like.' Everyone stopped eating and looked at me.

'So what did you do?' Dad asked.

'Nothing,' I said.

'Usually works,' he said and turned back to his plate.

'Might work but it doesn't fix prejudice,' Mum said in her stern voice.

'Mum, it was about the horse and Vicki's clothes.'

'Is that what you think?'

I just stared at my plate.

'They don't mean much by it,' Mum said gently. 'But it's still there. Mr Marriner said you did well. You and the horse.'

Good old Mr Marriner.

I left the table and since no one asked me to clean up or help with their homework, I got out of the house as quickly as I could and wandered down to the riding school. Maggie saw me coming up the lane and ambled over.

'Hello Maggie,' I said as she rammed her face down against my neck, nearly knocking me over. I could feel her eyelashes flicking against my skin. 'I should have bought you an apple or something. I wasn't thinking.'

I looked around the yard and saw the old tree against the barn where wart apples the size of big walnuts grew every year and no one ate — except the horses. I walked across, picked two and held them out to her one at a time on the flat of my palm. She rolled them with her lips before picking them up in her teeth and crushing them. When she finished she plucked at my shoulder with her lips and we stood there for ages. I turned to face Maggie and her eyes were closed.

'Thank you, Maggie. You're my best friend. I love you.'

With her smell still thick in my nostrils, I slipped back into horse dreams and the adventure to the river. Who could I ask to come? I couldn't ask Indie or any of the girls from pony club who had stood by in silence, but I could ask Tracey Burgess and Maria Giannarelli. It turned out Tracey was playing netball and Maria's horse had a sore fetlock. I didn't want to ask anyone else in case they said no. I didn't want to be disappointed. When I told Mum, she said my brothers had to come with me on their bikes.

'*Bikes*? Those two creeps on their *bikes?*'

'Look, you haven't ridden that horse much. You don't know how Maggie will go in the bush. What if she throws you? It'd be hours before anyone found you.'

‘She won’t throw me. Nothing scares her, Mum. She’s the quietest horse I’ve ever ridden.’

‘Ronnie and Eric are going with you.’

‘We’re going to the footy … ’ Eric whined.

‘You are *both* going with your sister after your game in the morning. I’ll pack some cold sausages, a bit of fruitcake and some drinks. Don’t look at me like that Ronnie. Dad’ll make up some lines so you can fish for mullet.’

You couldn’t argue with Mum when she got like that. She’d just go on and on. And so much for the adventure with my brothers hanging around. The boys sulked out of the room and the flywire door slammed behind them.

‘You can leave just before the boys come home from the game and I’ll send ’em off after you. You won’t even see them until lunchtime unless something happens. I know what you had in mind but I don’t want to end up like Mrs Arnold — a horse and no daughter.’ Mum looked at me hard. ‘Marnie, there will be other times when those girls will be able to go with you. Most of them have never ridden outside a paddock. They probably are not allowed to go bush by themselves. Oh, and by the way, you can drop a parcel off to Aunty Veronica on the way. You’ll be able to ride up past their house and show your cousins your new horse.’

There was something in that. Although I wanted to let my cousins know I had a horse, all this business of bikes, brothers and family was taking the fun out of it.

Eight

The science lesson droned on and on. Normally I would have been fascinated but today I had different thoughts in my head. It felt like it had been the longest week of my life. I couldn't stop dreaming about going to the river with Maggie. And I kept thinking about pony club and what Mr Marriner had told me about Indie and her dad.

I saw Indie at school and of course she ignored me. She had that expression on her face which I'd always assumed was a sneering pride. But now I saw her in a different light. I wondered if it was a look of doubt instead of self-assurance.

'And how does the Southern brown tree frog attach the spawn to weed, Marnie?'

My teacher's voice jolted me back to reality. Mr Manifold looked at me over his glasses. He had asked me because I usually knew the answers about animals. I froze and stared back blankly. I could hear the kids moving in their seats.

'Marnie Clark doesn't know for once,' cried one of the boys.

Mr Manifold swiftly directed the question back to the rest of the class. He wasn't a bad bloke. He always treated us Aboriginal kids fairly, even if he did go on about the importance of the first settlers' wheat and wool. And Mum said it was his ancestors who had taken the land from our old people.

At lunch I sat with Maria Giannerelli and we talked about horses as usual.

'I heard they gave you a hard time at pony club.'

'It wasn't that bad,' I said, hoping she'd be satisfied with that answer.

'How did Maggie go?'

'Perfect, got around the course no worries.'

'They won't forgive you for getting that horse, you know.'

'Course I know, I just don't want to think about it.'

'Wish I could come with you tomorrow.'

'You said Blaze had a sore fetlock.'

'He has. Anyway, Mum said she won't let me ride down to the beach on my own.'

'You won't be on your … ' I began and stopped short.

Maria looked down at the lunch she was eating and picked at it. 'Yeah I know but no one rides in my family and they think I'll have an accident or something.'

We looked out over the oval to where the boys were tackling each other playing footy.

'Mum's making my brothers come with me.'

'But they'll go off on their own,' she said. 'You wait — you'll be out riding without anyone telling you how to do it. I can't even look at my horse without Dad or my brother telling me how to ride … even though they wouldn't even know how to put their foot in a stirrup.'

We sat there until the bell rang and all I could think about was tomorrow.

Nine

When I got up in the morning, I could see that it would be fine. It was going to be a good day, brothers or no brothers. Mum must have been up for at least an hour. The food and drinks were packed in a saddlebag that Dad had found at the tip and sewn up with heavy fishing line. He'd even given it a good coat of saddle soap. It looked, well, not new, but it didn't look too bad. Every now and then one of his repair jobs worked.

I promised Mum I wouldn't leave before eleven o'clock so that the boys wouldn't be too far behind and I didn't. Well, not that much earlier. Ten thirty is nearly eleven o'clock. This way I'd have the whole river to myself, call in at Aunty Veronica's and still be able to get down to the beach and wade Maggie in the surf before the boys got there.

Some days you can tell when things are going your way. Just as I trotted Maggie out of the gate and across the creek, Mr Marriner came into view with his class of beginner riders walking their ponies in single file. They were just in time to see me jog Maggie through the shallow water, sending a shower of spray from each plunging hoof and then her great legs surging and striding up the opposite bank. I knew we must have looked good. I gave them a big wave as I cantered off down the creek track. I wished I'd been wearing a leather hat so I could have given a big salute to Mr Marriner but if he saw me without my helmet, he would get angry. He hardly ever got angry but when he did he was fierce — a man with no teeth always looks fierce when he yells.

As I passed the houses on the creek bank down near the bridge, my maths teacher from school looked up from weeding his tomatoes. I imagined him saying, 'That's Marnie Clark on a horse. Wow, what a goer!'

Crossing the bridge, I met three kids from school who stopped riding their bikes so that they could watch me riding past. I felt magnificent.

I held my breath as Maggie stepped off the bridge and onto the clay slope leading down to the riverbank. This was always tricky for horses but Maggie's feet just seemed to clamp her to the ground like giant clams. And very soon came the part I'd been dreaming about all week. The track from the bridge, to the river's entrance and on to the sea was one long winding trail that passed under wattles, mint bushes, gums, banksias, pittosporums, tea trees and paperbarks. The smells that drifted up off these trees were exquisite. I knew that no matter where I ended up in my life, that I would remember this moment as being close to perfect.

The track was firm but damp and Maggie's hooves made a rhythmic sound like someone whacking a hot water bottle with a stick wrapped in lamb's wool. I could hear it echo faintly off the trees on the other side of the river. It sounded like a ghostly rider was keeping stride for stride with me on the other bank. It was freaky, exhilarating and totally magic.

The leaves from low branches lashed at my helmet and made me feel as if I was going a hundred kilometres an hour. Maggie was starting to feel the pinch after weeks of being idle and her breath was coming in great deep gusts. *Hurrumph, hurrumph, hurrumph, hurrumph.* All I could hear was the mighty sound of galloping feet, her gusts of breath and the leaves whipping at my helmet. I felt strong and brave, like a warrior. It didn't matter about my brothers and the parcel for Aunty Veronica. This was the best day of my life!

Ten

I wheeled around Aunty Veronica's gatepost and sure enough, at the sound of the horse trotting up their drive all the kids came out.

It would have been more dramatic to toss the parcel onto the verandah and canter off in a shower of gravel but I'd never hear the end of it from Mum. And anyway, Maggie's chest was heaving and sweat was lathering her flanks. She could do with a rest and a drink.

Aunty Veronica bustled out onto the verandah as my cousins fought with each other to see who could get a bucket of water the quickest. In the end I had to give them all a turn sitting in the saddle and my little three-year-old cousin's eyes popped open like saucers when Maggie gave a huge snort into the bucket. She sounded like an angry dragon.

'Oh, Marnie what a beautiful horse!' said Aunty Veronica. 'Stay there and I'll get you a drink. You must be thirsty. Go around into the shade, love.'

I led Maggie into the shade. I didn't really want a drink but there was no stopping Aunty. I was about to sit on the verandah step when a voice startled me.

'I seen that horse before.'

I whipped my head around. I knew that voice. It was like a whistle from a leaky kettle — high pitched and moist. It was Uncle Binny's. I relaxed. He was sitting on the verandah with a cup of tea in his hand.

'Yeah, I know that horse. Belonged to the girl that died,' he said.

'Yes, Uncle. Her mum gave it to me.'

'Good horse,' he whistled through his teeth.

'You see that eye?' He pointed at Maggie with a knuckle the shape of an old artichoke.

'Maggie's eye?' I asked.

'Mrs Whitlam that horse, she got a real name you know.'

'I know, Uncle.'

'Well, you see that eye? It's a woman's eye. And we all come from women.'

I listened carefully, wondering what he would say next.

'You know that owl?'

'Which one, Uncle, there's a few.'

Uncle Binny was looking at me closely. I was holding my breath.

'That little owl, the woman one.'

'That nightjar, Uncle?'

'Yueh, the little one. Same as that horse, look … woman eye.'

I looked at Maggie's eye and felt a quiver go through me.

'She look after you, that horse, she got that woman eye.'

'Um … she's a good horse, Uncle.'

'I know,' he said matter-of-factly.

'Do you want another cup of tea, Uncle?'

'Sick of tea. All tea here … you got anything else?'

'Sorry, Uncle.'

'Yeah, me too. Sick of tea. Be good, my girl, look after that horse, you know when she hungry or wanna drink … need a kiss. You look 'em that eye.'

'Yes, Uncle.'

'Woman eye. Him first eye.'

I looked at him.

'First eye, woman always first. That's the lore.'

'Uncle Binny,' Aunty shouted from inside the house. 'You want another cuppa?'

'You tell her my girl, and don't forget to mention that this Elder would appreciate another type of beverage every now and then.'

'I heard that,' Aunty said as she walked onto the verandah. 'It's eleven o'clock in the morning!'

'No, it's not, it's the eleventh hour.' The wizened and buckled little man winked at me.

'Don't worry about him, Marnie. He reads the paper every day and thinks he's Einstein.'

Uncle Binny's shoulders were quivering like he was about to sneeze and that's how his leaky-squeezebox laughs always started. Aunty started to huff but then broke into a giggle herself. She nudged Uncle Binny on the shoulder.

'You old devil,' she muttered and gave him his cup of tea. He looked at it as if it was cod-liver oil. They both laughed.

One of my cousins came running around the corner with a bag of apples and it was hard to tell which one he was. They all had the same shirts, shorts, thongs and haircuts. When people asked Aunty Veronica about it, she'd just laugh and say, they knew who they were.

'Thanks for the apples! Maggie'll love them. Gotta go, Uncle, Aunty.'

'Say goodbye to your uncle properly,' Aunty Veronica said.

'Sorry, Uncle. Goodbye.'

'That all right, my girl, I enjoyed the yarn, took me mind off the tea.' He winked at Aunty Veronica who *hurrumphed* at him. 'You keep an eye on that horse and she'll keep an eye on you.'

Maggie leaned down and rubbed the sleeve of Uncle's shirt with her floppy lips.

'Best you get going,' said Aunty. 'Before there's more nonsense coming from this old man.'

Eleven

I walked Maggie back down the river track and trotted her gently through the low beach scrub to where the river entered the sea. Maggie set her ears forward when she heard the surf and smelt the sea, and she looked even more magnificent than ever.

I unsaddled her beneath a great banksia, which bowed down low into the bowl of a sand dune and made a perfect picnic grove. You could see the surf crashing through a gap in the bowl. Apart from a woman playing in the sand with her children, the beach was deserted.

I rubbed down Maggie's great barrel where sweat under the girth strap had matted the hair. She turned around and played with my ponytail with her rubbery lips.

'That feel pretty good does it Maggie?' I got out a towel and gave her a quick rub down to get the sweat off her hide. I took my helmet, shoes and socks off and led Maggie down to the surf. She wasn't keen on all the crashing surf or the foam of the breakers but she allowed herself to be led in it up to her hocks.

I splashed some water under Maggie's belly and could tell that she wasn't sure that this was sufficiently dignified. Gradually she relaxed and let me get on her bareback and urge her into deeper water.

Maggie lifted her hooves up high and smacked them back through the surface of the water, making huge splashes. Soon we were both drenched. Lucky I was wearing my bathers.

Where the river entered the sea, the water was quieter and I gently pressed Maggie into deeper water until she was swimming. What a sight we must have been, my magnificent horse plunging into the river with huge watery leaps until she found herself swimming, me astride the horse, revelling in the sensation of … of riding a whale. That's what it felt like. Fantastic. Surreal.

I slipped off her back into the water. Maggie even let me hang on to her tail while she swam around in circles towing me behind her. Nothing, absolutely nothing was better than this — and if the other girls were here they probably wouldn't have been able to get their horses to swim and I wouldn't have known the sensation of playing like this. Maggie wasn't afraid of anything and neither was I.

Back on the shore, Maggie rolled in the sand and then shook herself with a gigantic shiver that sent sand flying off her coat, mane and tail. She was enjoying herself, we both were.

Twelve

My mind decided my stomach was hungry. The thought of wood smoke and sizzling sausages made my stomach growl. Despite myself, I began wishing my brothers would arrive.

I looked up the river track but could see no sign of them. Perhaps they'd stopped off at Aunty Veronica's first. There were some surfers out near the reef but apart from the mother and the children playing in the sand, the beach was empty.

The mother had one child by the hand and was walking towards the water's edge. Suddenly she let out a wail which made the hairs on the back of my neck stand on end.

'My baby, my baby!' she screamed and instinctively looked over to where I was standing with Maggie.

I scanned the river but could see no sign of a child. The mother looked up and down the river and dashed to where her other child was standing by the water. She was frantic. I could see she just wanted to bolt into the water but couldn't leave her other children.

I looked out over the river again and along the bank hoping to see a little kid building a sandcastle or playing.

Something caught my eye close to the far bank. It could have been a plastic bag and I willed it to be one. I was scared of what I would have to do if it wasn't: knowing that the mother would look into my heart. Just a plastic bag, I muttered to myself but then I glimpsed a tiny hand rise above the surface.

Recent rains had created a swift current in the river and I could just make out the baby being carried towards the sea.

I let go of Maggie's rope and plunged into the river. The current dragged at my clothes and I swam as fast as I could so that I wasn't swept downstream. When I got within a few metres, I couldn't believe it was a real child. It was like someone had thrown a doll into the water.

The doll-child was floating on his back with his arms outstretched. His eyes stared blankly up at the sky and his skin … his skin was the colour of a pale stocking stuffed with cotton wool. Even as I reached out for his arm and pulled him towards me, he felt like a rag doll — completely lifeless.

I didn't have time to think and this was no doll. When I stopped to lift the baby, my body sank and I had to kick with all my strength to get going again. I was being dragged down by the current and I had to force my face out of the water to breathe.

I struck out for the closest shore knowing I had no hope of getting back to the mother. I could feel myself tiring and my legs screamed for a rest. I towed the little boy, battling the current and lifting his face out of the water.

I had this horrible feeling I was about to spew. I thought I was losing my grip and would have to let go to save myself.

The river current was stronger closer to its entrance into the sea. I thought we'd be swept out and I couldn't imagine being able to hold on for much longer. I wanted to cry and scream for Mum and Dad. It felt like I was being pulled under. I took another mouthful of water and coughed and choked.

The water bucketed along as it crossed the sandbar into the sea and there was no hope of swimming anywhere. I knew I was going to have to let go of the baby and the thought of the mother's eyes froze my heart. I was going under, pulled down by the turbulence, the dead weight of the baby and my own exhaustion when I felt something beside me.

At first I thought it was the child's mother but then I heard a muffled snort and realised it was Maggie. Exhausted, I grabbed her mane. She found her feet on the sand and lifted us clear of the water. Within seconds, Maggie was dragging us onto the bank.

The mother was beside herself with panic. She was separated from her baby by the river, not knowing whether he was dead or alive.

'Thank you, Maggie, thank you, girl,' I gasped as I lay the boy down on his side. My chest was heaving. All I wanted to do was collapse and get some air but I cleared the baby's mouth, making sure nothing was blocking his throat. The things you learnt at school!

The resuscitation steps came back to me as I pressed down on his tiny chest. Water escaped from his mouth. I cupped his chin and breathed slowly into his mouth, willing him to take the air from my lungs. Nothing else mattered. I could hear the mother screaming, 'Is he all right? Is he all right?'

She had sunk to the ground, beseeching me, afraid by her son's stillness. Her other children stared, terrified by their mother's wailing. Her yells had attracted the attention of the surfers out near the reef. They had caught the next wave in and were bounding through the shallows.

The blueness around the boy's mouth was beginning to scare me, and the grey colour of his skin made me wonder if I was kissing a dead baby.

'Hey Marnie, let me help you. We learnt lifesaving at surf club.' I looked up to see George Costa standing over me. George was one of the popular boys at school and someone I would never dare to say hello to.

'Have a rest,' he said calmly as he kneeled down. 'Just give his chest a pump every second breath I do ok? Gee, you did a great job. We could see you from our boards as we were coming in.'

He breathed into the baby's mouth. The baby blinked slowly. George breathed into the boy again and suddenly he spluttered and cried out.

'This kid's gonna live, Marnie!' George cried.

I pumped the baby's chest one last time, surprised that George even knew my name.

'Now get your horse because we're going to have to get this kid across the river.'

And that's what happened. George swam beside us and I straddled Maggie's back, tightly holding on to the baby. One of the other surfers swam ahead to tell the mother to get her car ready in case she had to take the baby to the hospital.

In the meantime, my brothers had arrived and had ridden back to Aunty Veronica's to ring for help.

George helped the mother get the baby and her kids into the car and they raced off to meet the ambulance.

I was left alone on the beach with Maggie. I sat down in the sand and burst into tears overwhelmed by the boy's face in the water. I couldn't believe I had saved him. Maggie nudged my face with her nose as if to say, 'It's all right, the little boy's okay'.

When my brothers came back, we all sat together on the sand. They raided my saddlebag and scoffed down the fruitcake and cold sausages.

'Here, you better have some,' said Ronnie, his mouth full. I didn't feel like anything. I just wanted to cry in Mum's arms.

Thirteen

They made a big fuss of me at home and at school. The mother brought the little boy around to our house to see me but I couldn't bring myself to look at his baby face. The last two nights I'd been dreaming about his staring eyes. He was beautiful, fair skinned and blue eyed now, not like the lifeless baby I had seen drifting down the river.

I was embarrassed when the school principal congratulated me in front of the whole school at assembly. I didn't believe I'd done anything out of the ordinary. It would be more difficult *not* to jump into the river when you saw a drowning baby!

And anyway, nobody thought to thank Maggie. Who knows how long it would have taken to get to the bank if Maggie hadn't swum across to me. Every minute was precious.

After that, every time I saw George Costa at school he gave me a big smile. He called me 'kid' even though he wasn't that much older than me. He would wave at me when I rode down the street, and even down at the beach he'd wave if I rode Maggie through the shore break. I kept on hoping he'd stop and talk to me but he never did.

'You thinkin' about the Golden Boy again?' Mr Marriner asked me one day as I brushed Maggie's coppery-red coat.

My face burnt with shame. Nothing much escaped Mr Marriner's notice. Some people called George the 'Golden Boy' because everyone liked him. He was a good surfer, was good at school and well, he did have golden skin.

'Don't be stupid!'

'How can I help it? He's a good kid but well … just be patient, girl, don't go growing up too fast! And don't go mooning after some boy without the brains and guts to match your own!'

If he was talking about George Costa he was sillier than he looked. I steadily ignored him.

Mr Marriner smiled as he walked off to the stables to muck out the soiled straw.

I brushed Maggie's coat until it blazed like hot copper in the sun. Maggie relished each of the strokes and closed her eyes in bliss.

One of the things that preyed on my mind after saving the little boy was the memory of Vicki. Mum had tried to talk to me but I didn't want to talk about it with her.

And of course, I was lucky. I had Mum and Dad, my brothers, cousins all over the place, close friends at school and a horse. Even some of the wealthier kids at school didn't have a horse. Perhaps their mums freaked out at the risk of them riding or their dads grizzled about having to find a paddock. Some fathers were hopeless at practical things. Dad could shoe a horse in thirty minutes. Mr Marriner had whistled through his teeth when he saw him do it the first time. 'One of the few jobs they let a blackfella have in the old days,' Dad said, packing up his tools. 'Pity they invented cars, man might still have a job.'

Fourteen

One afternoon, I was sitting on the beach watching Maggie roll in the sand after her swim in the breakers, and heard footsteps crunching behind me. I turned and blinked into the glare of the sun to see George Costa staring at me.

'Hi, how are you going?' he asked.

'Fine,' I replied in the calmest voice I could manage. I was too shy and nervous to think of anything else to say.

'I still feel strange about this part of the beach, you know. Don't you?' I simply stared at him. 'I haven't been able to forget that boy's face when you pulled him out of the water.'

'Yeah, me too. I can't even look at him,' I replied.

'Yeah, I'm kind of embarrassed when I see him or his mum.'

'Yeah, it's kind of like it's a different kid,' I said, as I continued to stare at him. I was hoping he wouldn't head off too quickly to surf with his mates. I could see them down near the river pulling on their wetsuits.

'When you got him out of the water, did you … did you remember how to do the resuscitation stuff? I mean I'd never thought about it since we learnt it at surf club and you sort of did it, straight away.'

'I thought about it while I was swimming. I was hoping I would get it right but mostly I was wishing it wouldn't be too late.'

'Yeah, I felt really strange until he started to cry,' said George. 'He looked funny, you know, like he wasn't real, like it wasn't happening.'

And finally I felt as if I was able to talk about it. I hoped we could talk more and that he wouldn't get too impatient. His mates were already paddling out to the waves.

'I didn't want to go out there, I just did it.'

'That horse of yours was pretty brilliant too.'

'Yeah, she's a real good friend.' What got me to say something as dopey as that to him? I felt myself go red in the face.

'Hey, you know, is your family ... um, is your family Aboriginal?'

'Yeah,' I replied, surprised by the sudden change in conversation.

'I thought you guys were Indian or something like that.'

'Nup, we're one hundred per cent Australian.'

'Well, my grandparents came from Greece. What does that make me?' he asked with a laugh.

I nearly said good-looking but stopped myself just in time.

'Um, do you want to come around for a barbecue to our place on Saturday?' He'd gone about as pink as he could go. 'It's my mum's birthday. She said to invite your family. So, do you reckon you'll be able to come?'

'Yes,' I replied. 'I reckon we will.'

'Oh good. We've got a pool. You could have a … '

'Swim?' I finished the sentence for him.

'Yeah. Anyway, see you Saturday.'

And he was gone. I watched him run off down to the water and grab his surfboard.

Wow, how did that happen? We have a conversation and then, boom I'm invited over to his house. How is that possible? The Golden Boy and me? I looked down and realised, to my embarrassment that I had my shirt on inside out. Well he still asked me out. To a barbecue. With my parents. And my brothers. I'd have to make sure that Dad didn't say anything daggy about the food. He was capable of saying anything *and* telling the most un-funny jokes.

Later, riding back along the river track, I made a point of stopping off at Aunty Veronica's.

'She's a nice kid that one,' said Aunty Veronica to Uncle Binny. 'Even if she's got her clothes on inside out.'

Fifteen

At the barbecue, George helped his father cook while Dad told them bad jokes and my brothers went feral in the pool. I spent most of the afternoon by the pool patting Zorba, the Costas' blind labrador. Not quite what I had in mind.

Mum was too embarrassed to swim around people she didn't know. Despite always telling us we were as good as everyone else and not to accept anything less, she spent a lot of the afternoon worrying about nothing.

Dad had a large collection of lame jokes, so I had half an ear on him hoping he wouldn't think they were hilarious by his third drink. I also had half an eye on my brothers as they were pretty much out of control in the pool.

George grinned at me every time he walked by with trays of cooked sausages and steak. It gave me a chance to look at his eyes again. A smile crept across my lips.

'What are you so happy about?' Dad asked as he appeared beside me. 'Still thinking about your photo in the paper?'

'I was thinking about Maggie,' I lied.

'Of course you were, I knew that. Just gammin ya.' He bent down and put an arm around my shoulder. 'I love ya Marnie from Killarney. And you got good taste in friends too.' He waggled his finger at me as he went back to the barbecue, intent on telling George and his dad another joke.

Zorba was nudging my hand to make sure I hadn't forgotten that his head needed patting. When I looked up, I got the fright of my life. Mrs Arnold was walking up the path with a bowl of fruit salad in her hands.

When she first saw me, she stopped in her tracks but then she walked over to Mrs Costa and they chatted for a while. Later I watched Mrs Arnold go over to where Mum was sitting.

I started to think I could sneak off with the excuse that I had to work to do at the stables but I was too slow. Mrs Arnold was walking towards me. She sat down at the pool's edge and didn't seem to notice her dress getting wet.

'Your mother thanked me for Mrs Whitlam,' Mrs Arnold said quietly. 'Mr Marriner told me how lovely you've been to the horse.' She paused. 'There's something else ... '

And just as suddenly as she had sat down, she stood up and hurried off down the path.

Mrs Costa watched her leave and then burst into tears. Looked like the party was over.

Sixteen

Crying must have been contagious. When I got home from school the next day, Mum was on the verandah, huddled on the old Holden seat, crying her heart out.

'Look,' she sobbed. 'She left this at the front door. I must have been hanging out the washing and didn't hear her come by.'

'Who? Who left what?' I asked Mum, confused.

Mum sat up and revealed the crumpled parcel in her lap. 'Mrs Arnold,' she sobbed again.

Mum ceremoniously pulled back the brown wrapping paper. Inside was a maroon velvet riding jacket. It took my breath away. I just knew it would match my dark blue velvet riding hat and Mrs Whitlam's coppery-red coat.

It. Was. Perfect.

AWARD-WINNING
Bruce Pascoe

Prime Minister's Literary Awards
Winner YA Fiction

Teacher's notes and more information
available from www.magabala.com

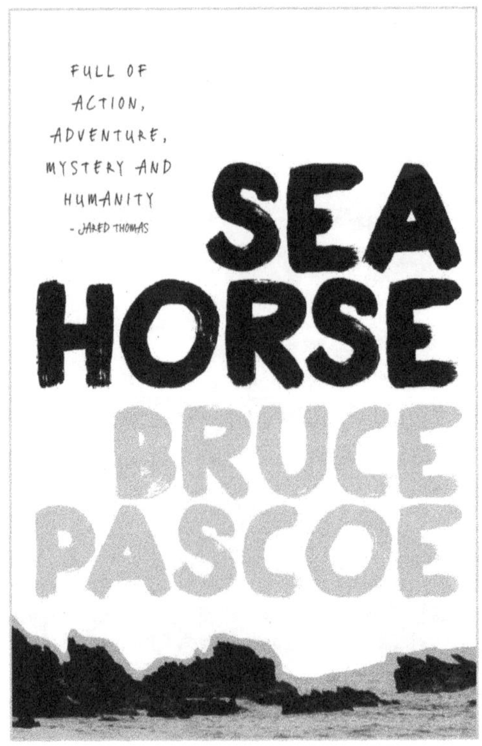

Teacher's notes and more information
available from www.magabala.com